# Short Stories for Seven-Year-Olds

Written by a 7 years old child who knows how to keep her age-mates hooked to a book!

This is a brilliant collection full of adventure and fun which will keep 7 year olds mesmerised.

Find out how a boy helped a baby Alien, a young Rabbit's adventure and how group of school kids took turns to have a good laugh.

Perfect for a self-read or to share.

This book is dedicated to our grandparents

All rights reserved @ Aleena Chattha & Talia Tipu

No part of this publication should be reproduced or transmitted in any form or shape or by any means without permission in writing by the writer

Written by Aleena Chattha
Illustrated by Talia Tipu

Cover & Interior designer
Robert Birkenhead at Charger Graphics

ISBN 9798681902911
Independently Published

# Contents

1. Baby Alien — P1
2. Fluffy the Youngest — P15
3. Hayden — P21
4. Turns to Laugh — P27
5. Being Invisible is Not much Fun — P33
6. Meeting Nellie — P39

# The Baby Alien

Tom can hear his Mum and Dad calling Tom, Tom! Slow down!!! and running to catch up with him but he only stopped when he reached the stream. Without even looking back he started collecting perfect stones for their 'Stone Skipping competition' one of his favourite activities in these woodlands.

While he was stuffing his shorts pockets with pebbles and stones Mr and Mrs Willow caught up with him. Mrs Willow was still panting after all that running but Tom didn't give her any time to catch her breath. He handed her a Shiny Big Bronze stone with a stripe in the middle and excitedly said "Mum I found a good luck stone for you. It will help you to win the competition." It made Mrs Willow smile she shrugged her shoulders and meekly said Tom.

Tom is full of energy and loves outdoor activities with his Mum and Dad.

Mum, Dad and Tom had a lovely picnic and afterwards they had their Stone Skipping competition, Of course Tom had to win. On the way home Mum said laughing (Can I throw the stone away?), it definitely didn't bring me any luck Tom, I still lost the competition!" Tom said "No Mum this is a special stone" and shoved the stone in his pocket. On the way home Tom continuously talked about the stone, how perfect and beautiful it was, they would never find such a stone again …."

They got home just in time for Supper. After supper Mum and Dad tucked Tom in his bed and asked him to sleep straight away saying "Tom, no story time today as we all had a long day and need some good rest now".

Tom was laying in dark thinking of what a nice day he had and staring at the most beautiful stone he has ever seen at that moment a strange green light flickered through the middle to the stone.  Tom couldn't resist calling Mum and Dad, He screamed "Mum, Dad come and see this". Mr and Mrs Willow came running to Tom's room asking "See what Tom?" Tom said "Can you see that green flickering light?" pointing towards the stone but looking at his Mum and Dad. "No" said Mum and Dad. Mum stroked his hair and said "Tom, it's time to sleep now, please". Tom couldn't believe it that light had vanished, he wanted to say that he was sure that light was there, that his parents should believe him but he kept quiet and just said "Good night".

After Mum and Dad went back to bed Tom stared at the rock for what seemed like ages hoping that the light would flicker again but nothing happened. Tom told himself "Tom you better control your imagination!"

But just then the Green light appeared again and slowly the stone started to open from the middle. Tom wanted to yell but no voice came out, his jaw kept dropping after he got a surprise after surprise. He rubbed his eyes and looked closely again and in the middle of the stone here stood the most amazing little creature looking straight back at Tom with an angry face.

The little creature started saying something in the scolding voice,"Zoo Zaa Zee Zoo Zee Zee Zoo Zaa "Tom said laughing and excitedly, "What are you saying Baby Alien?" The creature was shocked and he pressed a button on his arm and tried again "I'm not Baby Alien I'm Zoo Zoo.This time Tom could understand him. Tom said "Okay, Zoo Zoo I am sorry to call you Baby Alien" but Zoo Zoo was not stopping he kept scolding Tom "First you hung me upside down then you brought me here, How on Zimitoo am I going

to get back? His tone changed from angry to crying, he carried on saying I have sent signals from that spot to my Mum & Dad to pick me up and now Mum and Dad will leave without me as because of you they won't find me at the right spot."

Now instead of laughing Tom was feeling guilty and promised Zoo Zoo he would do anything to help. Tom crept downstairs climbed on a chair, got the keys, opened the door and he whispered to Zoo Zoo. "We are going to find your parents." Tom has never been

out alone in the dark before ,he had his torch with him but he was still scared.

His heart was pounding but he tried to sound brave "Zoo Zoo we'll be there soon!"

On way to forest Zoo Zoo told Tom all about his world and how they got on Earth on holidays and how Zoo Zoo was left back on Earth when he left on his shuttle to explore Earth without telling his Mum and

Dad. He was also worried about Tom as Tom was doing what Zoo Zoo has done not listening to his Mum and Dad and taking risks. They were soon talking like good friends.

Finally, after some walk, they reached the spot from where Tom has picked up Zoo Zoo's shuttle. It was 11.55 pm on Tom's watch just in time Zoo Zoo's parents' spaceship to land, they were supposed to pick Zoo Zoo exactly at 12 a.m otherwise the window

in Sky from their planet would close and they won't be able to come until next window is available and who know when it would be available again. It was 11.57 p.m and both friends were worried that Zoo Zoo's Mum and Dad won't be coming after all. But after 2 minutes a huge spaceship appeared in front of them with a flash of Green light.

Two slightly bigger Aliens came out and greeted Zoo Zoo with Zig zee zaz zee....... they all seemed to be happy. Zoo Zoo told Tom that they have been keeping them invisible as they didn't trust Tom but then they had to take a risk to take Zoo Zoo back in time. They had to rush back to reach their planet so they said bye to Tom.

Okay Zoo Zoo, Tom said if you visit earth again do come and play with me. Zoo Zoo was worried about Tom that he had to walk back in dark so he said something to his Mum and Dad like "zee za zoo zee…." And turned to Tom."We'll drop you back home on the way to Zimito".

**What a night it was Tom not only met Aliens and but had a ride on an Alien Spaceship!!!**

# Fluffy the Youngest

It was a warm breezy day when Fluffy's Mum asked her to get the juicy Orange Carrots from the Caroul Farm. Five months ago, they moved into this small house on the small farm which is more peaceful and safer. The best thing about it is that Fluffy can steal the Carrots without her five big brothers protecting her. When she reaches the farm, she realises she has already stolen all the Carrots from Caroul farm's small carrot patch, she has been here every day and she took some extra carrots everyday just in case she wanted a mid-night snack! She thought for a while to explore other vegetable patches but thought to herself "Mum said carrots so I should get carrots!" This is not the only farm here and I am big enough to go and get some from that Big Farm!" she went on an adventure to a Big Farm which was some 15 minutes hopping away and wow there was a huge carrot field there, not a path, **a field**!! Fluffy was so excited she was already thinking of words to explain her family how big the farm was, while thinking of how to tell her adventure tale she kept eating carrots and ate a lot of Carrots so she had to had a snooze after all that eating.

Suddenly she was woken up by a loud bang! She said to herself why is it so dark? She started running towards home but couldn't go anywhere as she bumped into something, she ran in other direction in dark and bumped again and then tried again and bumped again. This is when she realised that she was trapped!

Her heart was beating faster than a Cheetah! She just wanted to be with her family. Fluffy heard some children quarrelling over Fluffy, one said" It will be my pet". The other said "No, I saw it first". "Go and get them cute friendly bunnies, there are so many of them, look that Brown one is so cute. The first one was not convinced she said "But I like this small fluffy Grey one more", the older child said "What about the Light Brown one there he is super cute!

The younger child said "Okay, first let me just see this one under the bucket again" and with that child picked up the bucket.

At that very time Fluffy heard her brother saying run Fluffy, run home. They all ran as fast as they could without looking back. Once home she hugged all brothers and said "Having five big brothers is not as bad as I thought!"

# Hayden

It was nearly the end of August and Hayden's Summer holidays. Hayden wakes up and peeks through the curtains and says" Yes! it's a sunny day and I am going to the park." She just can't wait to try her new BMX which is her 7th Birthday gift by Mum and Dad.

She runs downstairs and looks for her parents in the living room. She finds her parents, her Mum was sitting on the sofa watching X- games.

Someone is skate boarding Mum cheers for the lady on the TV screen. Hayden has never seen her Mum so excited ever before in her life.

She had breakfast in front of TV, Hayden thought to herself "Mum must like skateboarding so much that she has allowed me to eat breakfast in front of TV", every time Mum shouts something

cool like, "What an acid drop" or "look at that flip!", Hayden wants to ask what Mum is saying and what she means, she has so many questions and she wants to enjoy it with Mum. Mum promises to answer all her questions but not during the competition.

They are so many shouts of Gnarly (Narlee) and Hayden quickly learns where to join in and she completely forgets her plan to try her new BMX.

Hayden is a little copy of her Mum deep blue eyes, straight blond hair which she usually tied in a high pony tail. She not only resembles her mum but she also shares a passion for outdoor activities.

-23-

Hayden is celebrating her 7th Birthday this weekend and suddenly she gets one of her ideas with a cheeky grin she turns and asks her Mum and Dad," Can I still ask for something else for my Birthday?" Mum smiled at Dad and he smiled back. They already know what she would ask for but still ask her what she wanted? Mum chuckled at her reply and said "Oh Hayden Can you please wait for a couple of months as you just got your new BMX bike?", but Hayden has yet to learn to wait.

The next day Hayden got very busy with her birthday party and a lot of new toys. Just then the doorbell rang (Ding Dong). Hayden ran expecting one of her friends but it was a postman holding a box just for Hayden, it was from her Grandparents coming all the way from Barcelona.

Inside lay an old rusty **SKATEBOARD** with a picture of her Mum when she was about her age. There was a Birthday card and it read "Dear Hayden, we are sorry we couldn't come over this summer to celebrate your Birthday with you, we hope you'll have a lovely day.

This is your Mum's, she got her very first skateboard as her 7th Birthday, she asked us to keep it safe for your Birthday and here is your first skateboard! hope you'll enjoy the sport as much as your Mum did."

Hayden was overjoyed she couldn't have asked for a better Birthday gift!!!

# Turns to Laugh

It was a beautiful Summer afternoon and the children of Summer Berry Primary School were enjoying their non uniform day. Daisy was sitting on the wooden bench near the Black berry bush, day dreaming about the lovely day it would be!

Suddenly, a shrieking voice interrupted her "Don't you want to look for your special thing in the bush?"

It was her classmate Tom, standing next to the bench with a cheeky grin on his face. Daisy was about to tell him off but before she opened her mouth her best friends Lilly and Sam joined her.

"What was Tom doing here?" asked Lilly. Daisy turned to Tom but he was gone, Tom and his friends were now standing at the far corner laughing at something looking towards girls. Daisy shrugged and said "I don't know!" and "I don't care" he is just being silly.

Ignoring them, they started looking for their imaginary Fairy friend, Lucy who lived in the Black berry bush.

All of a sudden, the girls started screaming and shouting "SNAKE!" "SNAKE!" and started running in all directions.

All the kids in the playground also started to shout and scream.

**Quiet!!!**

All of a sudden, all the playground went very quiet, No one even moved as if they were all statues only their heads turned towards where the voice came from.

Standing next to the bench was Mrs.Dale with her broad frame, curly blond hair and dark glasses. She was the strictest teacher in the school. Mrs. Dale snapped "what's the matter girls?" In a shivering voice Lilly said there was a Snake in the bush.

Mrs.Dale went behind the bushes to have a closer look and came back with a LONG, SCALLY, PLASTIC SNAKE!

Everyone could hear chuckles from the far corner of the playground where Tom and his friends were standing trying to control their laughter.

Mrs Dale slowly turned around to look at boys who immediately stopped laughing and they knew what was coming.

Boys you all have got a warning!" shrieked Mrs. Dale. Now it was the girls turn to giggle. They laughed all day long discussing the days' events.

# Being invisible is not much fun

Lily wakes up early in the morning in her bottom bunk and shouted excitedly, "wake up Jake, It's Good Friday!" Jake rubbed his eyes sleepily and heard lily called his name as she climbed up the ladder. Jake exclaimed that he was already up, but it seemed like Lily couldn't see or hear him as she completely ignored Jake and ran down stairs calling his name.

OH' Why can't she hear or see me? Jake questioned. Wait! I think my wish to be invisible came true last night. Last night at dining table Mum and Dad asked Lily and Jake what they most wished for? Jake was annoyed with Lily for not letting him play his games all Saturday so he immediately said "I wish to be invisible so that I can play whatever and Lily won't bother me!!" Lily got upset so Mum and Dad said "Jake you should always think about what you wish for, sometimes wishes come true."

Jake got very excited at idea of being invisible and he ran downstairs saying "I'm going to test this out". Lily was in the kitchen trying to fix herself some breakfast, she took Milk out of fridge and turned to get her cereal out of the cupboard.
Lily was startled to see her chair untucked and milk missing when she turned back. She opened the fridge

and was surprised to see the bottle of milk there. Jake was enjoying being invisible, when Lily tried to sit, he pulled her chair back a little bit more and Lily fell down.

She started screaming and calling Mum and Dad. When they came, she told them what was going on, she told them about the "Ghost" in the house, first it moved the things and then it made her fall down by pulling her chair back. As they comforted her, Jake chuckled. Now he was really enjoying being invisible and was already thinking of his next trick on Lily when Mum said listen Lily, "Almond is going to the funfair today with Grandma, Do you want to go too?"." Yes mum!" Lily excitedly said. Almond is Lily's and Jake's favourite Cousin and they always have fun plans for weekend together. Jake excitedly said "Can I go too?" and suddenly remembered that his family can't see or hear him as he is invisible when Mum, Dad and Lily carried on with their plans, Mum said "Lily get ready as Grandma is coming in half an hour".

Jake felt very upset that his mum didn't think about him and wished to be visible again. He was about to cry when his mum turned around, gently stroked him and whispered "Oh Jake you can go too". Then everyone started to laugh. "What you could see me?" asked Jake." We could see you all along!" exclaimed his giggling mum. Lily was laughing so hard that she couldn't even talk.

# Meeting Nellie

The door bell rang at number 131 Oakland Cottage. Mr Hue gets up from his rocking chair and slowly moves to answer the door but bell rings again, "I am coming!!!" he shouted and opened the door. Standing in front of the door were Mr Peter with his children. They all looked very excited. Mr Peter said "Sorry we didn't mean to rush you", shaking Mr Hue's hand he introduced himself and his kids "I am Peter and these are my children, I called you earlier today to come and have a look at Nellie.

Mr Hue turned and called "Elizabeth! Mr Peter is here to have a look at Nellie!", Mrs Hue walked to the hallway with tears in her eyes and said "Why don't you take them out and I'll join you later?"

Mr Hue led Mr Peter and his children at the back of the cottage, the kids were half walking and half running it was time for them to see Nellie. WOW!!! she is brown with a white mane, Perfect!!! Shouted 10 years old Scarlet at first sight of Nellie.

Nellie which was gracefully standing near the gate of her pen uttered a loud Neigh and ran towards the far end.

"Scarlet, you don't scare the animals like that" Mr Peter told Scarlet in a very stiff voice. Then he turned to Mr Hue and said "Sorry she is a little bit too excited to have a horse of her own."

Mr Hue said, "it's Okay, ever since our granddaughter Ellie has moved to America Nellie has been acting a bit anxious around strangers. Elizabeth and I have decided to sell her as we cannot take her out for riding anymore." And he then added in a bit grim voice "we think she misses Ellie as much as we do!"

Mr Hue started whistling and calling Nellie to calm her down but Nellie was now circling the Pen. The more he tried to calm Nellie the more anxious animal was getting and Mr Peter and his children were silently looking and waiting.

After 10 minutes fourteen years old Harry who was a bit bored by now gave a nudge to his Dad and whispered "Dad should we go home now?" Mr peter gave him a warning nudge back without saying anything. Harry got his message and moved back after putting on his head phones. Scarlet on the other hand got very interested in Nellie and started asking Mr Hue a lot of questions about her and Ellie.

-41-

When did you buy Nellie Mr Hue? Why did Ellie go to America? Was it a coincident the Ellie and Nellie had rhyming names?

Mr Hue gave a little laugh and said, "You are just like Ellie very inquisitive?" He was about to tell her everything about but at the very moment Mrs Hue came, she seemed to be more calm now and Mr Hue turned to Scarlet and said "Elizabeth would be more than happy to tell you everything while I try to get Nellie so that your Dad can have a better look."

Mr Hue was right, Mrs Hue started her story with a smile on her face, "Well Ellie always loved horses ever since she was a toddler and every evening we would take her to a nearby farm so that she could have a look at horses in the pasture and she always pointed to a beautiful light brown young horse with a white mane and would say 'I want this one!' When Ellie was 4 Years old, we decided to gift her.

'Nellie' the horse she loved so much as a Christmas gift. Nellie had been with Ellie for 10 years before she moved to America with her parents who wanted to work there for few years, she would come here to see us and Nellie every evening after her school. We miss her ………

Their conversation ended as Mr Hue came out of pen with a very clam Nellie saying "Here guys meet Nellie." But when Mr Peter came near to have a closer look and stroke Nellie, she raised her front legs and Neighed loudly. He quickly stepped back and said to Mr Hue "Maybe we'll come back some other day but he didn't sound as if he meant it". He turned to kids and said " come on kids your mum would be waiting for supper". Harry who was already looking forward to leave immediately started walking to the front of the house but Scarlet kept standing and staring at Nellie who was calm again and said "Stop Dad!! We don't have to buy Nellie today or take her home, I am sure Mr & Mrs Hue won't mind me coming here in evenings to get familiar with Nellie before we decide to buy her…… please Dad." She turned to look at her Dad and then Mr & Mrs Hue.

Mr & Mrs Hue who were looking bit sad smiled and said "Why not Scarlet you are welcome to come over even if you don't want to buy Nellie." Scarlet turned to her Dad Mr Peter who just wanted to leave said "Mr Hue that is so much appreciated it would give Scarlet some time to think if she really wants this horse, Thank you."

So that month Scarlet visited Nellie, Mr & Mrs Hue at Oakland farm everyday and by the end of the month she even had her first ever ride on Nellie.

Finally, the day came when Mr Peter pulled the horse box to Oakland farm to take Nellie to a pen, they have hired to keep Nellie near their house. It was a sad day for Hues they were saying good bye to the horse they had for over 10 years but they were happy for Nellie that she had found a new friend in Scarlet.

Scarlet was very excited but when she saw the tears in Mrs Hue's eyes she turned to her Dad and said, "Dad, I am sure Mr and Mrs Hue won't mind if we hire their pen and keep Nellie here?" Mr Peter turned to

Mr & Mrs Hue and started saying "I am sorry, you don't have to really, Scarlet is just a child full of ideas……." But both Mr and Mrs Hue smiled back and said "Oh, we would love that, we love having Scarlet here and this way we are able to see Nellie around as well."

Mr Peter turned to Scarlet who was looking at him with an innocent smile waiting for a 'Yes', he gave a meek smile and said "Well, I think a yes would make it a win win for everyone"

Nellie gave a loud happy Neigh as if she understood the whole conversation and as if she was saying that it is a win for her as well!

Printed in Great Britain
by Amazon